FRIENDS FUR-EVER!

2009

Town Teddy & Country Bear
A Classic Aesop's Fable Retold

Reverie

PUBLISHING COMPANY

Town Teddy &

First Edition/Third Printing

To purchase additional copies of this book, please contact:
Reverie Publishing Company, 130 Wineow Street
Cumberland, MD 21502
888-721-4999
www.reveriepublishing.com
Library of Congress Control Number 2004091635
ISBN 978-1-932485-19-6
Printed and bound in Korea

Country Bear

For Jack,
my husband, creative partner
and best friend

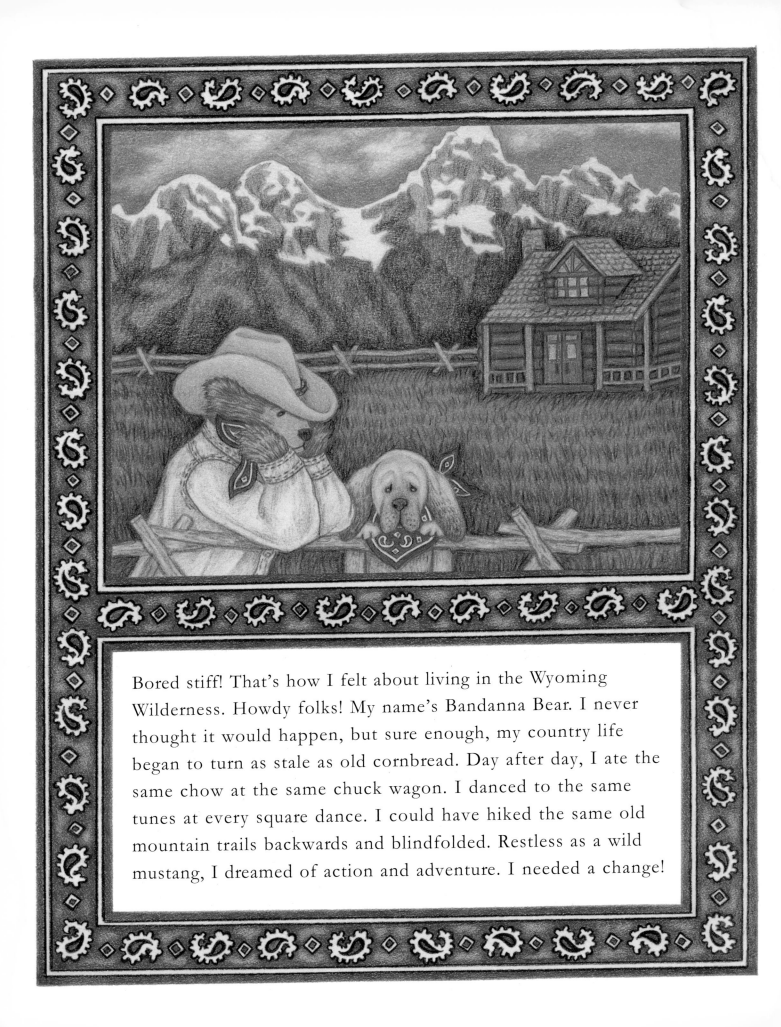

Bored stiff! That's how I felt about living in the Wyoming Wilderness. Howdy folks! My name's Bandanna Bear. I never thought it would happen, but sure enough, my country life began to turn as stale as old cornbread. Day after day, I ate the same chow at the same chuck wagon. I danced to the same tunes at every square dance. I could have hiked the same old mountain trails backwards and blindfolded. Restless as a wild mustang, I dreamed of action and adventure. I needed a change!

Utterly overwhelmed! That's how I felt about living in New York City. Pleased to meet you. I'm Bandanna's cousin, Tuxedo Teddy. I never thought it would happen, but my city life began to feel as hectic as Times Square on New Year's Eve. Crowds scurried everywhere like mice in a cheese shop. Concrete streets paved over every last blade of grass. Bright lights dimmed the stars. All stressed out, I dreamed of sunshine, fresh air and wide open spaces. I needed a change!

I was just about to give up hope of ever finding action and adventure when I met Cousin Tuxedo at our First Annual Family Reunion. He was singing the blues about his busy city life. "New York City has too many museums. Too many restaurants. Too many concerts. Too much of everything!" All that Tuxedo complained about was exactly what I hankered for!

When I first met Cousin Bandanna, he was bellyaching about his boring country life. "The country is so quiet, you can hear the cows graze. My neighbors live miles away. And there's nothing to do at night but count stars." Everything Bandanna complained about was exactly what I craved! We could each have our heart's desire if we just swapped places. Right then and there, we exchanged house keys and took off in opposite directions. We would each get exactly what we wished for.

The New York City skyline rose on the horizon like the peaks of a king's crown. Twinkling lights sparkled like diamonds. The Big Apple was a treasure chest just waiting to be opened. The action and adventure I dreamed of would soon be mine. Yee Haa! This country bear was about to become a bear about town!

The mist lifted from the Grand Teton Mountains like the curtain at the start of a Broadway Show. Sunshine beamed between jagged peaks. The rugged countryside was a playground just waiting to be explored. The great outdoors I dreamed of would soon be mine. Fabulous! This city bear would soon be at home on the range.

New York City streets were classy, but they weren't calm
like the country roads back home. Rush-hour traffic crawled
down Fifth Avenue. I drove my jeep up Fifth Avenue. I never
did see that "ONE WAY" sign. Beeping buses, careening cars
and tailgating taxis aimed straight for me! Darting through
traffic like a salmon swimming upstream, I knew I wasn't in
Wyoming anymore!

Wyoming's winding country roads were scenic, but they weren't numbered like the streets in the city. Soon I was lost in a maze of fields, farms and ranches. As I swerved around a curve on Rattlesnake Road, my screeching tires startled a herd of grazing cattle! I never noticed that "CATTLE CROSSING" sign. Racing ahead of the raging stampede, I knew I wasn't in New York City anymore!

Tuxedo's apartment was as fancy as a movie star's mansion.
All tuckered out, I slipped between the silky sheets. Clamping
a pillow over my ears couldn't drown out the ruckus outside
my window. No wonder they call New York "The City That
Never Sleeps!" If I could just get some shut-eye, I was sure
tomorrow would be a much better day. I couldn't wait to
take my first bite of the Big Apple!

Bandanna's cabin was as rugged as a wrangler's ranch. Utterly exhausted, I climbed under the patchwork quilt. There wasn't a sound except for the soft breeze whistling through the aspen trees. As much as I had yearned for peace and quiet, the silence sounded lonely. If only I could get a decent night's sleep, I was certain tomorrow would be a much better day. I couldn't wait to explore the great outdoors!

The next morning, the ancient treasures at the Metropolitan
Museum of Art drew me like a bee to wildflowers. The
Egyptian mummies looked so real, I just had to reach out
and touch one. Alarms shrieked...whoop! whoop! "Tumbling
tumbleweeds!" I pulled back my paw as if I had touched a
hot kettle in a campfire. Totally embarrassed, I smiled
sheepishly as I made my way to the exit. Stuffing my paws
in my pockets, I shuffled back to Tuxedo's apartment.

The next morning, the Snake River dared me to run its white water rapids. The raft rolled up and down the waves like a reckless roller coaster. Each time it splashed in the raging river, I was soaked with icy spray. Adventure soon turned to panic as a huge wave washed me overboard. "Goodness gracious!" I lunged for the life preserver and was reeled in like a fish on a pole! All washed up and worn out, I trudged back to Bandanna's cabin.

I closed the drapes in Tuxedo's apartment and pulled my hat down low. Nothing was turning out like I planned. What if I bit off more of the Big Apple than I could chew? Maybe a good hot meal would calm my frazzled nerves. New York City was famous for its gourmet grub, so I figured I might as well dig right in.

I slumped in the swing on Bandanna's porch, hoping the sun would dry my soggy fur. Nothing was turning out like I expected. What if I just couldn't rough it in the rugged great outdoors? Perhaps a hearty meal would perk me up. Wyoming was known for its "stick to your ribs" country cooking, so I simply had to indulge.

The menu at "Le Stuffed Bear Bistro" was written entirely in French. I couldn't read a word! Since I was chowing down in a fine French restaurant, I ordered the only French dish I knew... French fries. The snooty waiter delivered my fries with a disapproving frown. When I dug in with my bare paws, I drew dirty looks from nearby tables. Guessing I had done something wrong, I figured I'd best head for the exit.

The menu at "Bubba Bear's Bar-B-Q" was scribbled on a chalkboard. "Grits" sounded as tasty as gravel. Was "Chicken Fried Steak" steak or chicken? My barbeque ribs were served without a knife and fork. All the locals were digging in with their paws. I could eat with my paws or not eat at all. Gooey, gluey sauce stuck to my fur and stained my silk bow tie. Finding myself in a sticky situation, I quickly found the exit.

Catching a cab in the pouring rain was tougher than roping a calf. Soaked through to my stuffing, I felt things couldn't get much worse! I thought about calling it quits, but how could I head home without taking in a big night out on the town? Since no taxis stopped for me, I hiked through the raindrops and puddles to Lincoln Center, the musical heart of New York City.

I just missed the stagecoach as it pulled away for the weekly square dance. Breathless from the chase, I felt things couldn't get much worse! I thought about abandoning country life, but how could I head home without attending a local shindig? Missing my ride, I had to hoof it all the way to the Merry Moose Country Square Dance, the high point of the week.

Inside Lincoln Center, the conductor bowed on the dark and silent stage. He waved his wand like a wizard casting a spell. Trumpets blared, drums rumbled and violins soared. "Yee Haa!" Rising to my feet, I stomped my boots and joined right in with my trusty harmonica. The audience glared in my direction, silent as scarecrows. Dismissed from the concert hall, I finally gave up hope of ever becoming a bear about town.

Everyone square danced to the tunes of "The Blue Grass Bears." Guitars twanged, fiddles wailed and harmonicas whined. I tried joining in, but I seemed to dance to the beat of a different fiddle! Everyone circled left, but I circled right. They zigged, but I zagged. I kicked up my heels, launching my loose loafer! It soared through the air and splashed right into the center of the punch bowl. Herded to the exit, I finally gave up hope of ever feeling at home on the range.

It finally dawned on me. This country bear just wasn't suited to the city. I missed my cozy cabin, the great outdoors and my laid-back country life. It was time to go back home where I belonged. I packed up my jeep and headed for the wide open spaces of Wyoming. I couldn't wait to meet up with Tuxedo. Together we would have a good ol' time, enjoying the best of the Wyoming Wilderness.

A bumpy western trail ride finally knocked some sense into me. This town teddy just wasn't cut out for the country. I missed my posh apartment and the creature comforts of New York City. It was time to return home where I belonged. Eager to pack my bags, I hurried my horse into a wild gallop! I was hanging on for dear life when I heard a blaring whistle and a loud "WHOAH!" It was Bandanna Bear to the rescue! And just in time!

Tuxedo greeted me like a long-lost cow who had just found his herd! It turned out he was having as much trouble getting along in the country as I was surviving in the city! I talked him into staying in Wyoming a spell so I could show him the ropes.

The very next morning, we hit the Lupine Meadows hiking trail. At first, Tuxedo had to sit and catch his breath at every log and boulder. But once I began pointing out all the wildlife and wildflowers, the miles seemed to melt away. By the end of the week, Tuxedo was blazing the trails and loving it. But as much as we enjoyed our visit in the country, Tuxedo insisted it was now time for us to visit the city.

Our first night in New York City, we strolled down the red carpet at the opening of a Broadway Show. At first, Bandanna felt as out of place as a cat at a dog show. But once I began to point out all the models and movie stars, Bandanna got swept up in the excitement. He tipped his hat and swaggered in his boots like a country music star!

When the curtain lifted, Bandanna could "bearly" sit still through the catchy song and dance numbers. I had to remind him to wait until the cast took their final bows before standing and cheering. Waving his hat, he hollered, "Yee Haa!" By the end of the week, Bandanna was a real theater buff. He even learned to cheer "Bravo!" like a New Yorker! But as much as we enjoyed our visit in the city, we knew in our hearts that it was time to part ways and return to our own lives, once and for all.

Relaxed as a pair of old blue jeans. That's how I felt about
being back home in the Wyoming Wilderness. The chow
at the old chuck wagon tasted paw-lickin' good. My table
had a view of the majestic mountains. And when I stomped
my boots and tooted my harmonica at the country square
dance, everyone cheered. Yee Haa! Bandanna Bear was
back home on the range.

Pampered as a prince in a palace. That's how I felt about being back home in New York City. The food at my favorite French restaurant tasted fantastique! My table had a view of the sparkling city skyline. And when I whirled across the dance floor, everyone applauded. Fabulous! Tuxedo Teddy was back in town.

Although their homes are many miles apart,
Bandanna and Tuxedo have remained close friends.
Every summer, Tuxedo visits Bandanna in
Wyoming to hike through the Grand Teton Mountains.
Every winter, Bandanna visits Tuxedo in
New York City to take in the latest
Broadway Shows. Together, they share the best
of both the Town and the Country.